WHIMSICAL TIMES IN THE MYSTICAL CLOUD

TRISHA MENON

ISBN 979-888555039-0

To be writing on this page, is really ***a dream come true*** for me! So, here's for all who have been *with me* and *for me*!

To, two of the most supportive, encouraging and inspirational companions I have ever got - ***my parents***, and thanks to ***my baby-sister too*** - for all the interest and ideas along the way!

I thank my *teachers, friends, grandparents, aunts*, and *sisters* who have always motivated me, and paved way for my dreams to come true! Thanks to *all* who have helped, and **happy reading :)**

♡♡♡

Contents

Preface *vii*

1. No Luck Yet! 1

2. The Tremendous Muddle 4

3. A Discovery Of A Sign Of Adventure! 7

4. A Frenzy Of Excitement 10

5. Entry To The Cloud! 13

6. The Sapphire Waves! 16

7. Past Troubles And Future Troubles 19

8. The North Blue! 22

9. An Adventure Is Foreseen! 26

10. Let's Go Adventuring! 30

11. So Far, So Good! 34

12. The Most Extraordinary End! 38

Preface

When we hear the word **adventure**, what do we think? We think it is something daring, brave, and courageous. What about people who have adventures? We think they all have adventurous names like *Huckleberry Finn* and *Tom Sawyer.* Well, they have had many adventures and are really experienced in this sort of adventurous business. There are many other people too...but we have to move on.

Now what do we think when we hear fancy and gorgeous names like *Cordelia* or *Elizabeth*, or anything for that matter. We often have a mindset that they are more to do with princess or girlish things, right.

Well, this is the story of a set of triplets, *Tiara, Kiara* and *Miara* who have fancy names but adventurous minds. They long to have an adventure of their own; let's listen to their story......and hope that luck happens to drive past their town!!!

1

No luck yet!

Winter had relaxed its grip and the world was waking to new growth, colour and sound. The colours of the spring shouted and sang- rubies and emeralds, sapphires and opals. Crocuses smiled their greeting and tulips waved as they pushed their ways towards the sun. On this blissful morning, a voice called out, interrupting the melodious symphony of the song birds.

"No luck yet, aye, lil' T?"

"There's plenty of time for the day to end and spring has just taken birth today. There will be luck, ol' Hum." Called back a voice. Old Humdinger was a the friendly, and well-known senior citizen, belonging to the small English village.

"As fiery as always, aye, lil' T." he said with a chuckle.

Tiara, one of our three heroines, called lil' T, had this conversation with the old buddy, almost every day, be it rainy, snowy or sunny. Each sister chose to go different ways to school and back home, as they found it too queer to walk in a bulk.

Tiara, Kiara and Miara are a set of triplets, living in a magnificent house called 'The Heaven'. Their father, Mr.

Silverstein, a gentleman, works for the '**Golden Gazette**', the popular newspaper. A tall, slim and good-looking man he is, and always supportive and encouraging towards the children. Their mother, Mrs. Emeralkin, was tall and slender, with shiny and glossy brown hair that swung rhythmically from slide to slide as she walked. She made varieties of jam, and shipped them all around England.

Coming back to the triplets, they were a pack of daring and brave girls, but they never seemed to feel that life was adventurous enough.

Tiara, one of the three sisters, was a young and pretty child of twelve, with a head of reddish curls, which cascaded down her back. She had merry maroon eyes, and a tiny rose bud mouth. She was very much short-tempered.

Next comes Kiara, who was a sweet-tempered and beautiful child with long blonde hair, that flowed over her shoulders. She had twinkling eyes that sparkled like diamonds and smiling lips, that shone.

Lastly comes Miara, a friendly and helpful child, who unlike her sisters, had unruly orange hair that looked like flames blazing around her head. She had hazel eyes that danced with laughter, and tiny lips that always wore a mischievous smile.

They had all riches, fancy gowns, sparkling tiaras, princess heels and glittering ornaments, but the triplets always preferred jerseys and jeans better. They were different in almost everything, but they shared one similar thought:

"Fanciness is always a hurdle or hindrance, when it comes to adventures."

"You can't possibly wear fancy gowns when you go hiking", Tiara would exclaim when someone would force a gown on her. "You can't wear princess heels when you go trekking", Kiara would moan when somebody would buy her heels, for presents. "You can't wear ornaments or make-up, when you go to the woods. The creatures would probably flee, frightened by our looks", Miara would say, as she knew, this statement would make their parents withdraw from the attempt.

The sisters were always mocked and teased by their friends, for wanting adventures, when they had everything else. But the triplets firmly believed that one day, they would have an adventure, the most exciting and nail biting one, and they kept waiting for it.

2

The tremendous muddle

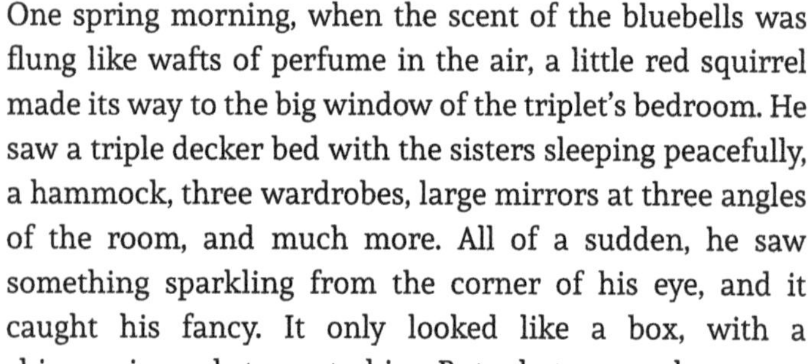

One spring morning, when the scent of the bluebells was flung like wafts of perfume in the air, a little red squirrel made its way to the big window of the triplet's bedroom. He saw a triple decker bed with the sisters sleeping peacefully, a hammock, three wardrobes, large mirrors at three angles of the room, and much more. All of a sudden, he saw something sparkling from the corner of his eye, and it caught his fancy. It only looked like a box, with a shimmering substance to him. But what was unknown to the squirrel, was that, it was a ring case. There were three ring cases, each holding rings, studded with a ruby, topaz and citrine for Tiara, Kiara and Miara respectively.

It was Tiara's ring case that was accidently left open, which caught his eye. He decided to get it for himself.

Luckily for him, Megan, the house maid, had just opened all the big windows of the household, due to which the sun poured in through the windows, and bathed the house in a brilliant light.

He popped into the room, and hopped out, until he reached his destination; the desk. He cleverly took out the ruby ring with his tiny front legs, and started receding, when he swung over the bed, he lost his balance and toppled over, making the ring tumble into Miara's pocket!

The squirrel jumped up in fright, and hopped up the bed. He softly padded over to Miara, with his cushioned furry paws, and touched her gently. Miara turned over, causing the ring to fall out of her pocket. The ring looked like it had lost its shine, but the squirrel scurried off with it hurriedly.

Little did the squirrel know that he had picked up the wrong ring, a dummy ring, specially prepared by Miara for a magic trick. So, when the real ring fell into her pocket, it got mixed with the dummy ring, which resembled the latter ring, and the squirrel mistook it for the real one.

Later the sisters woke up, and began to get ready for breakfast, when the busy bustling noise of the house was interrupted by a shrill piercing shriek, that echoed around the house. Kiara and Miara soon crowded around Tiara who was blinking in horror at her empty ring case. She considered her ring as her lucky charm. "Where on earth has it gone? It couldn't have just disappeared. I've lost my lucky charm; I'll never get it back...." moaned Tiara.

"Come on, we'll find it for you, it's not lost", assured Kiara.

"It's not like it walked off, we'll find it for sure" said Miara soothingly. Little did she know, that the very ring was safely tucked in her pocket.

"Whatever on earth made you scream like that? You gave me such a fright" asked Megan in her chirpy sing-song voice as she bustled into the room with hand in a bowl of pumpkin paste. Miara went into her sudden fits of laughter, looking at the short and plump jovial woman wobbling over, with her apron smeared with egg yolk and bacon rinds. Miara held her sides, tired of wiping the tears of laughter that came trickling down her cheeks, upsetting her ring in her pocket that tumbled into the bowl of pumpkin paste! Megan walked back to the kitchen, to finish her pumpkin pie, not knowing that the paste contains not only pumpkin but also the ring.

The family sat down at the table for breakfast, with Mrs. Emeralkin consoling Tiara in her voice as sweet as syrup. Soon the family were tucking into fried bacon, sausages and tomato rolls, cold ham sandwiches, and of course, pumpkin pie! Peaceful silence was hovering around until a surprised gasp was heard from Mr. Silverstein.

"*Oobo, oobo, oobo*!" he tried to speak. He had been marvelling and enjoying the pumpkin pie, when all of a sudden, everyone saw a bump on his cheek, as he tried to shift the substance from side to side. Finally, an exasperated Mr. Silverstein took a tissue paper, spit out the substance, and threw it in the waste bin, before he knew what he was doing. No one knew what it was, except Megan, herself, who went pale as she slowly knew what she got a glimpse of!

"Wait, wait! Don't throw it, Oh bother! But I have to take it out" saying so, she poked in the bin hastily, and he eyes widened she caught hold of the folded bit of tissue. She unfolded it immediately, and held out with pride, the ring, like it was an award!

Tiara lunged forward at once, and made a violent grab for the ring, but in her excitement, she lost her balance and landed with a thud! and the ring went flying out of the window!

"Now look at that! I lost my lucky charm and my luck!" she scowled in dismay, and with that she walked out of the house, *in a temper*!

3

A discovery of a sign of adventure!

Tiara walked along the familiar roads, then took a short cut to her dad's farms and fields. As she crossed the flower beds and ponds, she began to loosen herself and become free. She saw the red blossoms that hung in masses from vivid green stems. The golden corn was splashed with red poppies and yellow gorse. The hedges were alive with splashes of red and bright orange berries. She began to sing with the joyful song birds, and dance with the squirrels and rabbits. It looked like nature was making merry with her.

She was welcomed by wave after wave of the gently nodding heads of daffodils. Soon, she was skipping and hopping and making her way across the fields. She reached a part of the fields, she has never been to, but by now, she was enveloped by the vivid, sparkling treasures of spring. She walked steadily on, not seeming to notice that she had crossed the fields and entered a forest.

The forest floor was a carpet of blue bells dancing in the breeze. The vibrant sights and sounds of spring had her totally engrossed and immersed. By now, she had wandered far from home.

All of a sudden, *click!* a nut fell on her head. That was when she came back to her senses. She had now, to paths to follow: one was the way back home, and the other was the path, behind the several bushes, whose leaves danced in the light breeze, with fruit, heaped like piles of jewels, in front of her. She decided to go ahead and explore.

"But I must leave something of mine on this very spot, so I remember my way back." She wondered, and left her velvet wristband behind.

She stepped forward, and tried to wriggle through the bushes, but it was impossible to move quickly through the spidery tangle; she felt the brambles and thorns tear at her arms and legs. She hurriedly backed out, and saw the bruises on her body, but she couldn't help it. She looked up, and saw the trees that were joined together like a crowd of vivid green umbrellas. She searched for an opening or a hole near the bushes, and after much effort, found two parallel hedges, resembling an entrance.

In a thrice, she squeezed through the entrance and a saw a labyrinth of rocks and boulders, but unlike other mazes, the rocks were only half as tall as her, so she could make her way across easily.

Once on the other side, she saw split, cracked and carved by the magic of nature, huge and hostile mountains, from which flowing cheerfully came the waterfall which looked like silky, watery stairs that whispered as it fell.

Tiara's sharp eyes noticed a rope which hung down on one side of the mountains. It was knotted at intervals, which made it easier to climb.

She reached the top, and what she saw, made her lean forward, her maroon eyes bright with interest and excitement. Her body tingled with elation.

She saw, in front of her, the most magnificent vision of probably the longest flight of stairs, that were made of a queer looking, blue gel. The stairs ended at the feet of possibly, the largest, huge and enormous cloud that, was mysteriously pink, making it look like candy floss.

She was now sure, this would be an entrance to the world of adventures, and with an unbearable gurgle of elation, she began receding. She went down the road, out of the rocky maze, threw the hedges, and rushed hurriedly back home, eager to share this with Kiara and Miara.

She left her wristband as a landmark, and sped off home.

4

A frenzy of excitement

Meantime, loads had been happening at 'The Heaven', her home.

When, in the morning, Tiara's ring flew out of the window, and she left the house in a temper, the red squirrel had happened to be wandering again. He had been clever enough to realize that the ring was a dummy. He was just about to flick it away, the real one landed at his feet. He took a good look at it, and finding it extremely shiny, he took it. He hopped over the lawn, then Tiara came marching angrily. He jumped out of his skin, and climbed up the nearest tree, which was close to the triplet's bedroom. By doing so, the dummy ring toppled over the branch and fell right into the bedroom, and onto Kiara's tummy – who had been swinging on the hammock. She looked at it in surprise, and then mistook it for Tiara's ring. She hurried off to show it to Miara.

The squirrel meanwhile, trembled and swung onto the other trees, but accidently slipped and fell down upsetting the real ring, which tumbled down on the freshly mown lawn. Miara, meanwhile had been searching for the ring everywhere, and finally flopped down on the grass, when the ring toppled in front of her, she ran to show it to Kiara. The two sisters ran into each other and fell over with a thud! and once more the rings flew away from their hands.

Frustrated with the never-ending confusion, Miara exclaimed, "Oh! You had to run into me, silly. Just when I found the ring too!"

"You found the ring? Rubbish! I found it, and I was bringing it to you. My dear, what a muddle", replied Kiara.

"Come on, what are you saying? You must have found a dummy ring; it couldn't be real. I found it", Miara protested. In a thrice, she remembered her hand-made dummy ring, and began fumbling in her pockets for it. Then, she looked up and said, "I think, we've been muddling ourselves with Tiara's ring, and my hand-made *dummy* ring"

Kiara stared at her in disbelief, her mouth opening and shutting like a clown fish. They began searching for the ring, in every nook and corner. After about an hour of tiring, and continuous search, they slumped down on the velvet carpet.

At this moment, they heard the door bell ring, and once they opened the door, they were almost knocked over by Tiara, who in her excitement knocked and bumped into everything. "Oh! I've loads to tell you, I've loads, really" exclaimed Tiara.

But the others, only half heard what she said, for they were astonished by her sight; her legs and arms had bruises on them, her hair was dripping with water, and she was mossy and dirty. At this moment, they heard a familiar bustling noise, and Megan, at once sent all three to hot, warm baths.

Once fresh, they all sat at the table for lunch, with Mr. Silverstein checking every morsel before he ate. All of a sudden, Tiara gave a squeal of delight and picked up her ring from under the table. After lunch, the triplets went to their room, and began exchanging news.

Tiara began her tale, and told the bit about the cloud, and finally added sarcastically, "Well, without my lucky ring, I managed to discover that that cloud, so let's see what happens **WITH** the lucky ring". Then, the three of them began discussing and planning about when they would go to explore the cloud.

Well, well! Now, they were going to have adventures!

5

Entry to the cloud!

The relentless and merciless, steady downpour of rain, which unleashed stinging waves of drops the size of bullets, the previous night, had faded away. The rain had passed, and beams of light tinted the clouds with blazing colours of red and amber. The morning light stroked the hedges and glittered on the dew-soaked leaves, and the horizon was aflame with the rising sun.

The triplets awoke, their faces bubbling with excitement, thinking of the adventures, they were going to have in the cloud. They gobbled down their breakfast, hurriedly picked up their picnic basket specially prepared for them by Megan, and skipped past the squirrel, who happened to be hopping about again, probably wondering about what new mischief or muddle he could create.

They were shivering with excitement and pumped each other's hand enthusiastically. Tiara led the way, the laughter lines at the edge of the eyes deepening, her cheeks glowing. "wow! I've never been to this part of daddy's fields. This is so cool!"

"Superb! The perfect hideout, perfect scenery, perfect everything! Come on, where is it, this cloud? How far is it?"

asked Kiara eagerly.

"Just a teeny-weeny bit more, honest! Just a teeny-weeny bit, not like before. We're just coming to the bush gate" answered Tiara. Then she stopped, and motioned to the others to stop too. Her velvet wristband was not to be seen. She stood blank for two minutes, and then gave a squeal of delight, "Look, there are the bushes, the bush gate, come on"

The three of them managed to squeeze through and hurried on through the rock maze. Tiara, showed them the rope on the mountain, her hands shivering with eagerness, with an enthusiastic look on her face. The other two followed closely, their eyes burning with excitement. They climbed up the rope, as fast as they could. Their hands slipping in their joy.

Finally, when they made their way to the top, they almost fell down again, in their amazement and surprise. They awed at the magnificent cloud, and gazed at the flight of stairs, which went up, up, up and so high, they thought they'd never make it up there. And, they were almost about to retreat, as the stairs were made an awfully slippery and smooth blue gel, which was annoyingly slippery, this day. The sisters would somehow manage to climb up the stairs, sometimes crawling helplessly on all fours, sometimes jumping at top speed, but they would come sliding down immediately.

One time, Tiara climbed up, and nearly reached the top, but missed a footing and slid down the stairs and right down the waterfall and onto the fresh, stickily grass. Rigid with fury, she bounded like a uncoiled spring, and was just about to spoil their excitement, in her anger, when thoughtful Kiara jumped forward, and swung her sideways exclaiming, "wait a second, I know how to climb up. Just a minute, there!" saying so, she gathered together some of the dark green grass, which looked mysteriously enchanted, that was sticking out from Tiara's dress. She tied it in heaps, under her foot, and stepped on the gel-stairs, and voila! She did not slip! She began tying grass to the other's feet, her face, a mask of determination. When they were ready, they began climbing on all fours, and finally reached the cloud. They were now, bursting with excitement. Miara held both of their hands and took a long stride ahead into the cloud.

For a moment or two, she felt it was quite a wrong decision, for she was covered in a veil of stinging mist, which seemed to be hugging her tight, with slinky, grey arms; she was trapped in swirling, brooding mist, which was like an icy breath. Her eyes searched desperately, for a light of some sort; she looked up, down and around but saw only coils of icy, frosting mist that blanketed everything like a padded quilt, and a bitter whirl of icicles that fell like daggers. She began groping around in the darkness, yelling her head out for her sisters, who unknown to her, were right beside her, experiencing similar agony.

6

The Sapphire Waves!

Almost similar to the shock they got when they stepped into the cloud, was the astonishment, when they accidently stepped out of it. At first, the sisters blinked at the dazzling blue light, after being in the intensely dark cloud, but later they began to blink at the vision, they saw in front of them. The roof, or ceiling, was made of a thick sparkling blue gel, shaped like crystals, which formed a dome-shaped roof.

"That roof looks very much familiar to me, but somehow, I keep forgetting!" Miara exclaimed.

"Yes, it looks like that igloo, we made in second form, as a present for the eskimos" Kiara replied. "No, no, it looks familiar, in another way, I just don't remember". Miara protested.

They looked beneath them and saw a replica of the roof, as the floor. They were utterly puzzled, and muddled when a lilting and musical voice echoed around them, "What are we doing here...oh! They're *just* kids. Well, however did they enter? Now, come here, come on."

They saw a tall, and slender maiden with beautiful blue eyes, sparkling like sapphires on her fair, oval face. Her wavy, sea blue hair was gathered on top of her head and held in place by diamond pins, that turned her hair into a sparkling tiara. She was dressed royally in blue silk, with a translucent cape, studded with crystals, which made her look like she had been adorned by the sea.

"Come on, girls, come here" she insisted, the words floating out of her mouth, as though she were speaking through velvet. She was surrounded by fairies, who motioned to the sisters to obey her. They cautiously stepped forward.

That latter introduced herself, after seating herself on the throne, with an air of prestige, "I, am the Princess of the Waters, the ruler of the 'Emerald Surface', the heir to the throne of 'Sapphire Waves', Princess Crystal". She added, "I absolutely dislike people who boast, but these are the last days of my reign, in other words, to remind myself of my royalty, is to show off, to **STRANGERS** like you".

Kiara was a bit shaken at being termed a stranger, and exclaimed in a hurt tone, "Well, Crystal, I mean Princess Crystal, we are not strangers at all, and we are very friendly and helpful. You can freely open yourself, for I can see, your hiding something from us".

Then, Tiara continued, "We are triplets, I am Tiara, and they are Kiara and Miara. We live quite far from here. Actually, we had always wished for adventures in our life, and when we discovered this cloud, we thought we might have an adventure. We never meant to harm anyone, nor to penetrate into anyone's life."

"Oh! Well, I never thought that the cloud would be so easily discovered. I had asked "Blue", my assistant, to keep it well hidden from the rest of the world. I had even carved a long flight of stairs, from the water gel we'd used for our palace, so that no one could arrive here due to its slippery nature. The only way to climb up the stairs is by using the enchanted grass that grows at the bottom of the silky stairs – the waterfall – anyway...." Princess Crystal explained.

"Well, now I know why the roof and floor looked familiar to me." blurted Miara, then smiled looking at everyone.

"Well, I think, I can confide in you three, for now, I know you are trustworthy. I shall tell you about the 'History of the Sapphire Waves'." said the Princess.

ఌఌఌ

7

Past troubles and future troubles

'The Sapphire Waves', was an enchanted kingdom, hidden in the depths of the ocean, ruled by the *Emperor Colossal*. Each drop of water was a magnificent house for the subjects of the kingdom. For long, the kingdoms of the waters and kingdoms of fire had battled with each other. During Emperor Colossal's reign of the Sapphire Waves, the kingdom of the 'Blazing Flames' was ruled by Emperor Fury.

The kingdom of the Blazing Flames was another enchanted kingdom, which was well protected and hidden in the depths of the Sun, where each spark of fire was a magnificent house for the subjects of the *Emperor Fury*, who lived in the heart of the Sun in his palace, the Blazing Flames. He was, as suggested by his name, extremely furious; he blasted and exploded everything that came in his way, due to which his subjects always trembled and shook at his arrival.

In the entire world, he deeply loved only one person, his sister, Princess Citrine. She was a replica of her brother, auburn hair like liquid copper, yellow hawk's eyes, and she had supernatural fire powers, but unlike her brother, she did not have a cruel heart, but gentle and kind manners.

Once, during an Aqua-Ignis war, under some circumstances, Emperor Colossal, captivated Princess Citrine. It was impossible for a maiden from the 'Blazing Flames', to enter the sea, in her fiery form, until she was married to one of the men, belonging to the sea, and since Emperor Colossal had attained a marriageable age, he wedded the princess.

This enraged Emperor Fury, so after few months, he waged a treacherous war the 'Sapphire Waves'. This time, he was not only confronted by Emperor Colossal, but also Empress Citrine, who had been cursed earlier, that she would defeat her brother in a war.

She unleashed all her igneous powers, and also released the '**Ash Smash**', a weapon gifted to her by her brother once. She unleased the mighty weapon at her brother, due to whose side effects, his face was disfigured by a hideous scar that ran the length of one of his face and pulled his mouth into a permanent snarl.

Once after this war, after years, she gave birth to Princess Crystal, who got the traits of her father, blue hair, blue eyes and everything. She was made ruler of the Emerald Surface, and heir to the throne. Her coronation was to be held on her eighteenth birthday. Princess Crystal was preparing herself for the coronation, two weeks before the big day, she already had the waters at her control, and possessed magical powers. By becoming Queen, she would get in her possession; the *Tiara of the Torrents*, with which she could create storms, cyclones, and stop them too.

Then she would get the *Ring of the Weathers*, with which she could control different seasons. Lastly, she would receive the *Trident of All Magical Worlds*, which would give her extra powers, and make her the most supreme, ultimate being on earth.

But, at that moment, their messenger came with a message from the Emperor Fury, which said that he was waging a war against them, which he had been master planning, for years. Moreover, it said that if they lost, they would have to give him the trident, and he could choose one more thing he wanted. Emperor Colossal, Empress Citrine and the Princess got ready for the war, armed themselves, and when the wartime arrived, they fought with great valour and bravery, but unfortunately, they lost.

Emperor Fury took his chance, grabbed the trident and captivated Empress Citrine too, as the coronation ceremony would need the presence of both the parents, and the absence of even one parent would badly affect the princess. Moreover, with the loss of the trident, the ceremony could not be held. The trident was locked with a powerful seal, which could only be broken by a universal spell, known only by Emperor Colossal.

So, Emperor Fury, safe at his palace, was busy forcing the spell out of Queen Citrine, who kept insisting that she knew nothing. Meanwhile Emperor Colossal, began preparing his soldiers for a colossal war.

Princess Crystal, kept sending her spies over and across the sun, and paced up and down her room restlessly.

Days passed, but everything remained the same, and her coronation neared. On one such day, was the triplet's arrival. Let's see what is going to happen now!

8

The North Blue!

Only after hearing about the past, did the seriousness of the condition dawn upon the triplets. They couldn't bear to watch the gloomy and downcast, forlorn face of the Princess anymore. The stifled sob of the Princess made an unbearably enormous sapling of determination grow in the triplet's heart.

"We will surely help you in whatever way we can, Princess, we shall definitely solve your problem for you" Miara declared.

"We may be kids, but it does not mean we can't help. We will not let another tear trickle down your face, Princess. Trust us, we are very loyal and honest", confirmed Tiara.

"We shall do whatever you tell us to do, Princess, be it waging a war, or battling against villains. We are at your command, Princess" assured Kiara.

You could confirm that the Princess was feeling better hearing this, for her face lit up in a big smile and her eyes shone like beams from a torch. "Oh! I do trust you three. Somehow, I feel that the saviours, I'd been waiting all time long for, are standing right in front of me." She exclaimed.

The triplets beamed, their cheeks glowing.

"But it is not as easy as you think. My daddy, keeps assuring me that the war he is preparing for, will be a most colossal one, and we will emerge successful. But I know that this is not possible......." The Princess was interrupted by curious Kiara who until then had been listening carefully," But why Princess? After all,..." Then she remained quiet, looking at everyone's faces.

"During the last battle, Emperor Fury had unleashed a long-lasting spell on all of our soldiers, due to which, they would lose half their strength. Though daddy says, he's been using all powerful potions to reverse the spell, I know that we will have no other way than to surrender to Uncle Fury." Then she added rather mysteriously," But my personal assistant, 'Blue', revealed another way to get the trident and mom, without ANY war or fight!"

"Why are you so downcast then? You can easily succeed surely." Asked Miara.

"I think there is a hurdle, Mia. Princess, please reveal the secret to us." Kiara thoughtfully said.

Princess Crystal motioned to everyone to be quiet, removed her glittering cape, and held it out in front of her. Then lifting her voice, she sang:

"Oh Spirits! Of far and near,
At my command you do appear!
Obey or follow, at a stroke or thought,
My magical spirits, forget me not!"

Much to the amazement of the triplets, she let go of the cape, and it began to float mid-air. A dazzling light, flooded the chamber, and just as mysteriously as it had appeared, the light faded. Slowly, the cape began to take the shape of a giant. But it didn't stop! It shrank smaller to form a human. It didn't stop still, and shrank smaller to form an elf. It shrank smaller and smaller, until it became just a flickering light, and finally exploded into a magnificent spiral of blue and silver light. When the light faded, they saw a small elf, who normally as a spirit would remain invisible to all, except the princess, but took the form of an elf today at the princess' request.

He indeed looked a strange sight, with his turquoise, shimmering hair like a wild, tangled stack combed and knotted by the fingers of the wind. His emerald, green eyes smiled impishly from under heavy, bushy eyebrows, and he gave an impish grin, while stroking his goatee beard with his tiny hands. The tight-fitting red, tweed vest and yellow jump-suit, striped with orange, looked very good on his short, and plump body.

He did a little hop, bowed low to the princess, and spoke in a rather queer manner, with his voice clicking away in an odd way," Wee, wee! Me princess, what can we do for thee?"

Princess Crystal laughed uncontrollably at the triplets who gaped at the elf. She commanded," Blue, look here! These are my new friends, Tiara, Kiara and Miara. They're trustable. I want you to reveal the secret to them, Blue. They are going to help us. Take us to the North blue."

The elf nodded thoughtfully, then raised his head, held the princess' and triplet's hands and began uttering some codes. As he spoke, a mysteriously, cold wind began to blow around them, and before they knew what was happening, they were transferred to another drop of water. It was not just any drop of water, but the one which was right under the sun. It was called the 'North Blue'.

The North Blue, was not only a chamber of secrets and legends, but also the entrance to the,' **Tunnel of the Shadows**'.

The triplets looked around curiously, and walked cautiously afraid of stepping on something dangerous. The

North Blue, was a small room, with portraits of emperors, scrolls containing legends, maps leading to places all across the sea, and much more, embedded on the spherical walls. There was an empty canvas on one side, which arouse suspicion in the triplets. The princess sensed this, and remarked mournfully, "These are the pictures of my ancestors. My dad's picture is there, and so is my mom's. my portrait was supposed to be here." She said pointing to the empty canvas. Then she cheerfully added," I'm counting on you three, to fulfil my wish."

The triplets nodded, and turned to Blue, who in the meantime, had pressed on a panel, causing it to move sideways, giving way to a small cupboard.

He opened the cupboard, causing the triplets to lean forward, their eyes shining with interest and excitement.

Let's see, what was inside!!!

9

An adventure is foreseen!

The cupboard contained four shelves, out of which three shelves held hundreds of scrolls. The first shelf, had a chest on it. Blue, let out a shrill, piercing whistle, due to which, the chest flew down to him as if in an answer. He opened the chest, and brought out a '**Scroll machine**'.

"You can insert a scroll in this machine, and a hologram would appear, revealing the secret of the scroll." The princess explained.

As she spoke, Blue pulled out a scroll, which was blue and golden in colour, and unusually bright making it look different from the other scrolls. The princess inserted the scroll and as explained, a hologram appeared, displaying the contents of the scroll.

"***Quod Secretum Modo,***" Tiara began to read the contents of the scroll loudly, to the others,"***Ignotum sibi esse imperatoris sui hosti clandestino!*** "

"Now whatever on earth does that mean?" exclaimed Miara.

"It sounds familiar.... oh! It's Latin. We learn Latin, but this sounds rather difficult to translate." Said Kiara.

"Wee, wee! It is revealing a secret that is unknown to the emperor himself," explained Blue, lowering his voice, trying his best not to giggle, at the children's confusion," It says that there is a secret path to his enemy's house, that originates from his kingdom, itself!"

"Wow! But, why didn't you use that idea. You could easily rescue the Queen, and regain the trident", asked Kiara.

"It is because", explained the princess, "the trip to the sun, will be a two-day trip. And if I disappear for two days, daddy, will want to know the reason, goodness knows what will happen. He never lets me near Uncle Fury".

"Two days? We would be obliged to complete this task for you, Princess, but, two days is just too long". Complained Miara.

"Moreover, if we disappear for two days, we'll have to reveal the story to our parents as well. What about that?" asked Kiara.

"Speaking of which, how do we, explain this 'half day absence', to our parents. How long has it been? We 've stayed for too long!" exclaimed Tiara.

"Oh! My Dear! My saviours, you must know that a minute in your world, is a day in our world. So, whether it's a four-day trip or a ten-day trip, it will just be a matter of minutes in your home. "Said the Princess.

The triplets, huddled together, discussed in low voices and then reported to Princess Crystal, "Triplets at your service Princess, we will do anything for you."

Then Blue started explaining to them, the way to the sun, "Wee, wee! The North Blue, opens to the 'Tunnel of the Shadows'. To get to the sun, u need to follow the tunnel, but beware of the dangerous barriers it produces. The tunnel opens to the 'Anemone of the depths'. Unlike the poisonous variety of sea anemones, the 'Anemone of the depths', is the largest anemone, with the bounciest, longest and also the stickiest tentacles. It can curl around you, and hold you within its tentacles for days."

"Don't scare them, Blue. " Exclaimed the Princess, "Nothing will happen to you, if you manage to befriend the Clownfish princess Jennilia. She is quiet, annoyingly irritable, but as I said, if you can bring her under your control, you can enter the anemone."

"Once you reach the middle of the anemone, it will compress and rebound, sending you fly high, so high, that you will land on the, 'Cliff of the Burning Embers.' The cliff is probably the largest crater, which smoulders ash and rocks, and is a cauldron of spitting bubbles, hissing steam and belching fumes. You can only survive in the crater for three minutes, and you have to find the 'Sizzling Stairs', in that time, else you'll be cooked in fire. "

"Come on Blue, you can be gentler than that, don't scare them. Once on the Sizzling Stairs, you will enter the palace of the 'Blazing flames. "Exclaimed Princess Crystal.

"Yes, and then you have to be extremely careful not to land in the hands of Emperor Fury. Are you ready?" asked Blue.

The triplets nodded instantly wide with excitement.

"You don't have to worry, for I will be with you, throughout the journey." Assured Blue, then added, "But I'll have to leave you, once you're in the palace, for, spirits can never enter the sun."

The triplets nodded, and bid farewell to the Princess, who looked far better now, her previously glassy eyes, now twinkling with hope. They returned home, whispering to each other excitedly, wishing for the next day to arrive.

The next day, the triplets set off to the cloud, the dawn's first rays marking a successful beginning for their adventure. Let's wish luck to the triplets!

10

Let's go adventuring!

The triplets, began leaping in the air, screaming with excitement; they could not believe that the day of adventure, they had been waiting for all life, had finally arrived. When they stepped in the cloud, they saw a rather miserable princess, with sadness enveloping her like a dark cloud. As soon as, she saw them, she walked towards them and said, "My saviours, all hope is gone. My daddy says that the soldiers, are too weak to fight, so he is deciding to hold my coronation, in three days. It has been preponed. The ceremony is going to be very precise and short, as mom is not present. He needs me and Blue for the preparations. So, that's that!"

"But Princess, we can manage without Blue, and the ceremony is only in three days. We'll fix it for you" said Tiara.

The Princess beamed, and asked them hopefully, "Well, do you think you can manage on your own, without Blue. If so, lets move forward without delaying it anymore."

The triplets were led, to the North Blue, and Blue pressed on a wall. It gave way, and opened to a dark tunnel.

"Let me warn you, for the last time kids. You have to be very careful." said Blue, and motioned to them to move forward. Biding a hopeful farewell, the trio set off. The tunnel, as suggested by the name, was resembling a silent, screaming mouth. The sisters sang loudly all the time, for they were afraid that at any time, they would lose each other.

"Oh! I would like to thank myself, for remembering to bring this kerosene lamp, as, if it weren't for this we would have got lost, long before." Kiara would say at times.

The tunnel sometimes would, become extremely low and narrow, and the triplets would often find it extremely annoying to hunch low, squaring their shoulders. Often, they would bump their head into the huge, spiky stalactites, and after receiving almost the fiftieth bruise on her head, Tiara shouted, rigid with fury, "Of all the necessities! We could have stayed home in our comfortable beds, instead of banging our heads into these sharp, pointed things. Bother the Princess, and horrible elf."

"Don't lose your temper and speak rude about the princess. We offered to help her right ..." Kiara said, and at that very moment she bumped her head into a spiky stalactite. She exclaimed, "Actually you're right. Blue could've accompanied us on this treacherous journey, he could've been a very useful navigator for us."

Miara walked ahead, ignoring the two of them and their argument, not realizing that the path grew slipperier, until the path gave way and she found herself slipping and falling down. She gave a yell and would have almost fallen down, if it weren't for her sisters' sudden and timely help.

The three of them, began holding hands and walked ahead overcoming all barriers when, they found themselves extraordinarily hungry. They sat down, on the cold stone floor, and helped themselves to the meat-pie, they had stollen from their larder. Once full they resumed their journey, and after sometime found the tunnel, had come to an end.

They found, half of the inner part of a large bubble projecting out, from the exit.

Tiara held both of their hands, and touched the bubble. It popped at once, and a colossal rush of wind took the triplets along with it, and led them far, far ahead until the sisters saw in front of them, an enormous, exquisite sea anemone. As astonishingly as it came, the wind left them, near the anemone.

Kiara awed at it, and ventured near, and would have nearly been caught by its tentacles, if she hadn't hopped aside. The sisters wondered what to do, when they heard a voice, smooth like polished glass, "Well, well! Three girls come to pay old Jennilia a visit! What are you doing here?"

The triplets looked all around themselves, and in a thrice, Tiara remembered about the clownfish princess, and how they had to befriend her. "A very good evening to you, your majesty." She said, in a most polite manner.

"It's good morning, not evening! Still in your dreams, huh, you girl?" came back the voice, turning rather unpleasant now. Tiara turned red, but sweet Kiara nudged her and said," My dear Princess, we are triplets, who have heard a lot about your majesty. We've heard you sing well." She added," Can we hear your sweet voice?"

The princess, obviously flattered hearing this, replied, "Why, my guests, you should have said that before. Come in, come to Jennilia."

She came outside; the anemone's tentacles gave way to her. They entered immediately; the Princess led them, to the middle of the anemone, which took a long time.

Finally, the triplets reached the middle. The Princess motioned to the sisters to get seated, while she closed her eyes and began to sing. As she sang, the sisters felt the anemone jerking slowly, and compressing itself. They held each other's hand and sat excitedly, until, with a great big sigh, the anemone rebounded, sending the screaming triplets fly up high, high, high and so high, that they only looked like specks, finally to the clown fish, who mumbled sadly, at having lost her company.

Now, wherever did the triplet vanish to? Let's see!

11

So far, so good!

The sisters thought, they would never land, as they were flying at a very high speed, indeed, such that everything around them looked like a blur; they could not make out whether they reached anywhere near a cliff, or a crater for that matter, when all of a sudden, Thud!

They landed on their backs, in a large crater. They sat about, struggling to get out, as they were overwhelmingly dizzy. They began to feel extremely hot and suffocated, when they remembered that they had to find the "**Sizzling Stairs**"!

The sisters began to desperately search everywhere for the stairs, coughing and spluttering. Every moment, the heat and suffocation grew more, and the search grew more extensive. In her fright and hurry, Miara tripped over something and fell on her face. She looked up angrily and then exclaimed, "Now, look here. Here are the stairs, we've been searching for, all time long. I think, they've been invisible until I touched them by tripping over."

It looked like a magical, invisible layer unravelling itself, revealing what it was hiding. A long flight of stairs shone like ember in front of them, gleaming in an orange light.

"I wonder why it's called the sizzling stairs", wondered Tiara, and stepped on the stairs. The next moment she knew why, for the stairs were so sizzling hot, she jumped down again. Then, she remembered about Blue's warning, and motioned to the others to follow her. The three of them began hopping and jumping up the stairs, howling in pain. The stairs ended at the foot of a large ray of light. The sisters leapt into it, and found themselves getting smouldered in humid air which coiled itself around them, and settled around their bodies. The merciless heat beat down on them, sapped all their remaining energies, and suffocated them in its intolerable steam.

They began running hither and tither, until they accidently stepped out of the ray of light.

They blinked at the surroundings, glad to get out of the heat, when they saw an extremely magnificent and marvellous palace in front of them, with guards patrolling it. At once, they hid behind a nearby a gorse bush, wiped off sweat from their faces, and huddled together to discuss about their next plan.

Finally, they decided to play a trick on the guards. They made a sound from behind the bushes, and when the guards came running towards the bushes, they stole to the entrance to the palace, laughing their hearts out, at the success of befooling the guards.

Once inside the palace, they began to hide behind pillars and tiptoe about. They had no idea about where they would find the queen of the trident. They peeked out from a pillar, and ducked back in, for they heard footsteps, and someone mumbled in a cracked old voice, "He had to hand the keys to me, *me*, and irresponsible old fellow. Whatever on earth am I to say to Fury?", saying so, he coughed dryly, and walked past the very pillar, the triplets were hiding behind. As he walked by, Tiara saw dangling from his belt, a pair of keys hanging from a shiny key hanger. The glittering keys caught her fancy, and she secretly took the keys. The old man, did not know this, and walked ahead. She put them in her pocket.

The triplets tiptoed further, and saw a large door embedded with rubies. They stood there, deciding what to do, when they heard a lady sobbing. They decided to open the door, but could not find any keys. All of a sudden, Tiara remembered about the keys she had in her pocket. She immediately tried them, one by one, in the lock, and the door opened. They closed it behind them. As soon as they opened it, the lady gave a cry of surprise. She jumped up, causing her auburn hair to get tangled up, and her yellow eyes gleamed with tears. She was dressed in fiery, red silk, and she wore a tiara. The triplets guessed that she was probably a damsel, locked up by Emperor Fury.

“Oh! Thank you for opening the door for me! I had no idea who you are, but you came just at the right time”, explained the lady, then she saw the keys in Tiara’s hand, and asked, “Would you mind, if I got those keys? I need them”. Tiara held them out to the lady, who grabbed them at once, then she turned back to the triplets. She inquired about their arrival. The sisters explained about how they had wanted adventures, found the cloud, understood about the current circumstance in the Sapphire Wave, and set out to rescue the Empress and the trident. The lady’s eyes gleamed when she heard this, but she said nothing, only nodded thoughtfully. The triplets trusted her.

The lady said that she had seen the trident being locked in a small room, and would help the sister, who gladly agreed. The lady led them to a room, and opened the door with Tiara’s keys. They climbed down the millions of dusty and rumbling stairs that they found unravelling in front of them. They went inside softly, and found a huge bell-jar with the most miraculous and brilliantly white trident, that was studded with precious gems.

The tripled awed at it, and the lady quietly took the trident, and motioned to the sisters to follow her. They quietly tiptoed out of the palace, when all of a sudden, they were confronted by a most furious Emperor Fury!

Uh-Oh! Let's see happens now!

12

The most EXTRAORDINARY end!

Emperor Fury surely looked furious, the scar looking absolutely frightening on his snarling face.

"Now, where do you think you are going, my dear? Or should I say, dears?" he asked in a gruff voice, with a thick accent.

The triplets were numb and paralysed by fear, shivers tore down their spines and racked their bodies. They expected the lady to tremble too, but she looked rather brave, courageous and at the same time furious. She raced to her full height, leaned forward menacingly, and then she, most astonishingly, stood still with a calm look on her face. This startled the Emperor, as well as the sisters.

The lady hesitated for a moment, then she stood, deep in thought. After a minute, she lunged forward, and then pierced the trident into the Emperor's body. Writhing in pain, he curled into a ball, and howled like a wounded animal.

The lady sank to the ground, her face shadowed with grief and misery. She spoke with tears in her eyes, "Fury, I wouldn't have had to do this, but I only had two options. Either the coronation ceremony, or your end. She has to become the Queen..."

The triplets were now utterly confused. Who was the lady speaking about?

All of a sudden Emperor Fury vanished in a cloud of smoke, and all that was left behind was the trident. The lady seemed happier now, and holding the triplet's hand, she grabbed the trident, swished it in the air, and in a thunderous echo and flash of lightening, they were transferred to the 'Sapphire Waves'!

When the triplets opened their eyes, they saw Emperor Colossal, Princess Crystal, and Blue.

Tiara said to the excited Princess, "We got the trident, with the help of a lady, who killed Emperor Fury, but Empress..." She added, "We couldn't find her". All of a sudden, the lady came out of the shadows holding the trident. Kiara was about to introduce the lady to them, when Princess Crystal yelled excitedly, "Mommy", and hugged the lady happily.

Only then did it dawn upon the triplets that the lady was none other than Empress Citrine. They stood blank. The Empress laughed and patted the triplets on their backs, and said, "Well, well! These are some brave kids. They are really saviours!" The sisters beamed in delight.

"You arrived just in time; my coronation is to be held in a few minutes. I am going to be Queen", exclaimed the Princess happily. Finally, it was time for the coronation. It was held in great pomp and show. All fairies, angels, sea-creatures, friends, relatives and subjects of the royal family, celestial beings and of course! The triplets were present for the coronation.

The best part was that, when the Princess was being adorned by the 'Tiara of the Torrents', the 'Ring of the Weathers', and the 'Trident of all Magical Worlds', at the Princess' request, the triplets were awarded with the **'Gems of Valour'**, mementos studded with the purest of sapphires.

Today, the sisters go back home; they are not fancy girls doing fancy things, but brave and courageous warriors who have had an adventure. They walked with an air of prestige, proudly marching with 'Gems of Valour'. I wonder what Ol' Hum will say, when he hears about this adventure from Tiara.

To everyone out there wishing for adventures, there will always be a red squirrel which will lead you to one.

For now, let's leave the triplets to their happiness, **a very big hug to you**, from ***Tiara, Kiara and Miara.***

9 798885 550390

Printed by Libri Plureos GmbH in Hamburg,
Germany